This
Amelia Fang
book belongs to:

Hope

I celebrated World Book Day 2020 with
this gift from my local bookseller,
Laura Ellen Anderson
and Egmont
#ShareAStory

CELEBRATE STORIES. LOVE READING.

This book has been specially created and published to celebrate *World Book Day*. *World Book Day* is a charity funded by publishers and booksellers in the UK and Ireland. Our mission is to offer every child and young person the opportunity to read and love books by giving you the chance to have a book of your own. To find out more, and for loads of fun activities and reading recommendations to help you to keep reading, visit *worldbookday.com*.

World Book Day in the UK and Ireland is also made possible by generous sponsorship from National Book Tokens and support from authors and illustrators.

World Book Day works in partnership with a number of charities, who are all working to encourage a love of reading for pleasure.

The National Literacy Trust is an independent charity that encourages children and young people to enjoy reading. Just 10 minutes of reading every day can make a big difference to how well you do at school and to how successful you could be in life. *literacytrust.org.uk*

The Reading Agency inspires people of all ages and backgrounds to read for pleasure and empowerment. They run the Summer Reading Challenge in partnership with libraries; they also support reading groups in schools and libraries all year round. Find out more and join your local library. *summerreadingchallenge.org.uk*

BookTrust is the UK's largest children's reading charity. Each year they reach 3.4 million children across the UK with books, resources and support to help develop a love of reading. *booktrust.org.uk*

World Book Day also facilitates fundraising for:
Book Aid International, an international book donation and library development charity. Every year, they provide one million books to libraries and schools in communities where children would otherwise have little or no opportunity to read. *bookaid.org*

Read for Good, who motivate children in schools to read for fun through its sponsored read, which thousands of schools run on World Book Day and throughout the year. The money raised provides new books and resident storytellers in all the children's hospitals in the UK. *readforgood.org*

AMELIA FANG

and the

BOOKWORM GANG

LAURA ELLEN ANDERSON

Ghoulish Greetings!

AMELIA FANG

AND SQUASHY

LIKES:
Reading about pumpkins

DISLIKES:
Running out of
story ideas

LIKES:
Dramatic tales

DISLIKES:
Bookworms

TANGINE

AND PUMPY

LIKES:
TOADSTAR comics

DISLIKES:
Homework

FLORENCE AND GRIMALDI

LIKES:
Nice calm poems

DISLIKES:
Tragic stories

COUNT DRAKE AND COUNTESS FRIVOLEETA

LIKES:
Trumpet dresses
and crosswords

DISLIKES:
Lost trumpet dresses
and incorrect
crosswords

KARL

LIKES:
Pushing wheelbarrows

DISLIKES:
Not pushing
wheelbarrows

MABLE

LIKES:
Pie Berries

DISLIKES:
Berry Pies

VINCENT

LIKES:
Throwing
mashed brain

DISLIKES:
Being quiet

To all of the wonderful libraries
who make reading possible for everyone

EGMONT
We bring stories to life

First published in Great Britain in 2020
by Egmont UK Limited
2 Minster Court, 10th floor, London EC3R 7BB

Text and illustrations copyright © 2020 Laura Ellen Anderson

The moral rights of the author and illustrator have been asserted

ISBN 978 1 4052 97639

A CIP catalogue record for this title is available from the British Library

70947/001

Printed and bound in Great Britain by CPI Group

CHAPTER 1

BRAINWASHED FLAMINGO FROGS

It was a dark and gloomy Friday night in Nocturnia. Young vampire Amelia Fang was engrossed in her favourite Nocturnian tale, *The Pumpkin Whisperer*. It was reading hour at Catacomb Academy and everyone was enjoying their favourite books.

'I love this book,' sighed Amelia, stroking a picture of a glowing white pumpkin. 'I wish I had magic like the Pumpkin Whisperer. I'd be able to heal poorly pumpkins with the touch of my hand.'

'THAT WOULD BE PRETTY COOL,' said her friend, Florence Spudwick, a large and very rare breed of yeti. 'YOU'D BE LIKE A

SUPERHERO, JUST LIKE TOADSTAR!'
Florence waved her comic book around and
prodded at a page with a picture of a caped
toad wearing a mask. 'IN THE "BATTLE
OF THE POND BEYOND" ISSUE,
TOADSTAR DEFEATS A WHOLE ARMY
OF BRAINWASHED FLAMINGO-FROGS!'

'Those comics scare me!' squeaked
Grimaldi, Amelia's little grim reaper friend,
as he floated around, scythe in hand.

'*I* don't think they're scary!' said Prince Tangine La Floofle the First, flicking his glittery hair. 'Although I don't understand why more books aren't about *me*! I AM half vampire-half fairy, and the most fabulous of them ALL.'

'CAREFUL, I FINK YOUR BIG 'EAD IS GONNA ROLL OFF IN A MINUTE!' said Florence as the others giggled.

The sound of the Catacomb Academy bones rattled through the classroom, marking the end of the school night.

'FINALLY, IT'S THE WEEKEND. ZOMBIE TAG TIME!' bellowed Florence, slamming her comic book shut. 'HURRAH!'

'CLASS!' called Miss InSpine, the skeleton headteacher. 'Before you go chasing zombies around the graveyard, I have some homework for you.'

'Ugh!' Tangine threw himself across the desk dramatically.

A dreary groan resounded across the room. Even the walls groaned.

'This homework will count towards your

Hallows Eve exam at the end of the school year,' Miss InSpine continued. 'I want you all to write your *own* stories . . . and then share them with everyone in Abominable Assembly on Monday night.'

As the bizarre bunch of creatures left the classroom, Miss InSpine tapped Amelia on the shoulder and smiled. 'I can't wait to hear what you come up with, Miss Fang!'

Amelia grinned and embraced her copy of *The Pumpkin Whisperer*. Amelia loved writing stories just as much as she loved PUMPKINS!

Outside in the Catacomb Academy graveyard, Squashy pa-doinged over to Amelia happily, waggling his stalk from side to side.

'Hello, you!' Amelia said, as the little pumpkin jumped into her arms.

Florence waved her *Toadstar* comic around excitedly in her large hairy paw. 'I'M TOTALLY GONNA MAKE UP MY OWN SUPERHERO STORY! WHAT ARE YOU GUYS FINKIN' OF WRITING ABOUT?'

'I don't know for sure yet,' said Tangine in

PA-DOING

deep thought. 'But I *do* know that it WON'T end happily. A tragic story with a hint of LOVE.'

'Not sure about tragedy, but the "love" bit sounds nice,' said Grimaldi. 'I might write a nice story about sugarplums or something . . . How about you, Amelia? I bet you've got LOADS of good ideas!'

Amelia tapped her chin and pondered for a moment. 'I'm not sure yet,' she said. 'But I do love writing stories, so I'm sure I'll come up with something.'

Amelia skipped to the Fang Mansion with Squashy bouncing behind her all the way. She was very excited to get back to her room and start writing.

5

Later that night, the grandfather clock BONGED time and time again as the hours passed by. The moon began to set, but Amelia still had NO idea what story to write . . .

CHAPTER 2
DANGEROUS THINGS!

At moonrise the next night, Amelia sat bleary-eyed in the kitchen, *still* trying to come up with a good story idea. She chewed at the end of her bat-wing pen and scribbled down notes but *none* of her ideas seemed good enough. Plus, it was a little tricky to focus when Amelia's baby brother was throwing handfuls of brain pie in her face.

'Vincent!' said Amelia as calmly as she could. 'Please stop that. You're meant to *eat* the food.'

She picked up his tiny spoon and scooped the food into his fangless mouth. Vincent spat it back out. Squashy bounced around under the table, delightedly lapping up all the food that made it on to the floor.

Desperately trying to ignore her brother, Amelia took a deep breath, dipped her bat-wing fountain pen into a pot of black ink and . . .

SPLODGE!

Another big blob of brain pie splattered across the pages of her notebook. Vincent gurgled in delight then sneezed, firing snot through the air straight into Amelia's ink pot. Black ink splashed *everywhere*.

Amelia's mother, Countess Frivoleeta ran into the kitchen looking flustered. 'I don't suppose you've seen my trumpet dress, have you? You know, the dress that looks like a trumpet?'

Amelia shook her head. 'No, sorry Mum,'

she said. 'I'm actually a little busy right now trying to write a story . . .'

'How exciting! You've always been such a disastrously delightful writer!' said the countess. 'What's your story about?'

'I'm not sure yet,' Amelia said with a sigh.

'Anything I can help with?' asked her mother.

'No thank you,' Amelia replied quickly. 'I should do this myself.'

'Well, don't be afraid to ask for a little help if you need it, my gorgeous little fart-fest,' her mother replied, putting an arm around her daughter.

SPLODGE!

More of Vincent's dinner landed on Amelia's notebook. Countess Frivolecta shook her head. 'Vincent! Stop tormenting your sister. Can't you see she's trying to do her homework?'

Amelia was wiping as much brain off her notebook as she could when a desperate cry echoed through the mansion. It was Count Drake, Amelia's father.

'WHAT THE BAAAAAAATS?!' he shrieked.

Amelia sighed. At this rate she'd *never* get her story written!

Count Drake came running into the kitchen, brandishing five copies of his *Crossword Critters* magazine. He slammed it

down on top of Amelia's notebook. 'There's an ERROR on the Petrifying Puzzle of the Week! AN ERROR. Frivoleeta, my awful little pint of armpit sweat, come and SEE!'

'Dearest little wart snipper, I can't,' Countess Frivoleeta replied, searching through the fridge shelves for her dress. 'I've lost my trumpet dress! You know, the dress that looks like a trumpet? It's Vincent's Fang-warming in six months and I need to get it cobweb-cleaned!'

'But this is devastatingly important, my grubby little pine cone!' urged Count Drake.

'Um, Dad,' said Amelia. 'Could you move your crosswords please? I have to write a story for my homework.'

'Oh! Sorry,' said her dad, retrieving the magazine. 'What are you writing about?'

'I'm not sure yet,' said Amelia, feeling exasperated.

'Maybe your ol' dad can inspire you!' Count Drake suggested, striking a funny pose.

'Thanks Dad, but I need to work this out myself,' said Amelia.

Vincent, meanwhile, was rubbing brain pie all over his face.

'No, no, no!' said the countess, taking the bowl away. 'Enough of that!'

Vincent began to howl. Since Vincent had been born, Amelia couldn't remember a quiet night in the Fang Mansion. She stood up quickly.

'I'm going to find somewhere a bit less *splattery* and noisy to write,' she said. 'Mum, Can I go to Loose Limbs Library to do my homework please?'

If anything was going to inspire her, being surrounded by lots of books would surely do the job!

'Oh, of course, my little drain of darkness. I'm so sorry about all the racket here,' said the countess as Amelia gathered her things. She kissed Amelia on the forehead. 'I promise it won't always be this chaotic. Vincent is just a bit cranky as his first fangs are coming through.'

As soon as Amelia left the Fang Mansion, she felt as if her ears had been switched off. A cool breeze hit her face and the smell of damp moss filled her nose. The faint groan of a trapped zombie resonated from the nearby graveyard, but other than that, it was quiet. It was nice. Amelia was SURE she'd be able to come up with a GREAT story once she'd got to the library. Squashy padoinged cheerfully beside her.

'HEY, AMELIA!' came Florence's booming voice from behind her. Amelia turned around and gave her best friend a big smile.

'WHERE YOU OFF TO?' asked Florence. She spotted the brain-splattered notebook in Amelia's hand. 'OOOH, DID YOU FINISH YOUR STORY?! CAN I 'EAR IT?! I JUST KNOW IT'LL BE AWESOME! YOUR STORIES ARE THE BEST!'

Amelia felt a little rumble of nerves. But she pushed it aside. She wouldn't be stuck on her story for much longer! She just needed to get to the library.

'Almost finished,' she told Florence as cheerfully as she could. She felt a bit bad for fibbing. 'I'm just going to the Loose Limbs

Library to get some inspiration, if you want to join me?'

'GOOD IDEA! SHALL WE SEE IF GRIMALDI WANTS TO COME TOO?' Florence asked cheerily. 'AND THE LIBRARY IS IN TANGINE'S PALACE, SO I'M SURE 'E'LL WANT TO JOIN US. WE'LL BE LIKE AN EPIC HOMEWORK CLUB! PLUS, WE'LL PROB'LY NEED YOUR 'ELP WIV OUR STORY IDEAS! HEHE!' She chuckled.

'Sure . . . you know me – FULL of *great* story ideas!' said Amelia, feeling her tummy flutter again.

She'd definitely think of something soon. Wouldn't she?

CHAPTER 3

LOSE THE PIE BERRY

Amelia, Squashy and Florence called for Grimaldi before making their way across the misty planes of Nocturnia to the Loose Limbs Library.

The Library was located in the West Wing of Nocturnia Palace, home to Prince Tangine and his parents, King Vladimir and Queen Fairyweather. They'd always said Amelia and her friends were welcome to use the library whenever they liked.

The gang was greeted at the very grand front door by an incredibly old mummy maid called Mable. She smiled sweetly.

'Hello, Tangine's friends!' said Mable. She waved and her ear fell off.

'Hi Mable!' said Amelia. She knew most of

the Palace mummy maids now. 'We've come to read some books in Loose Limbs Library!'

The mummy maid squinted and tapped the side of her head. 'Speak up, dear!' she croaked.

'Can we come in and use the library please?' Amelia said, a little louder.

'Lose the pie berry?' asked the mummy maid. 'Why would I lose the pie berry?'

Florence stepped forward. 'CAN WE COME IN PLEASE?'

'The plum king cheese?!' said Mable, looking confused. She shook her head and ushered the friends into the palace entrance hall. 'I'll go and find Tangine for you, and then I'll see if I can fetch some plums for the king's cheese.' And she shuffled away *very* slowly.

Deciding that it might be some time before Tangine was summoned, Amelia, Florence and Grimaldi made their way through the palace to the West Wing with Squashy bouncing cheerfully alongside them. But when they got to the library, a long black ribbon was draped across the wooden doors.

'Looks like the library is closed,' said Grimaldi.

Amelia frowned. She *really* hoped this wasn't the case. She needed to find inspiration in the library. If not, she wouldn't be able to write her story! She scooped up Squashy and knocked hopefully on the door.

'Hellooooo? Is anyone in there?' she called through the keyhole. 'Can we use the library please?'

But nobody answered.

'LEMME TRY,' said Florence. She bashed the doors with her big hairy paws.

BAM BAM BAM BAM!

Nothing.

Suddenly Amelia thought she heard something shuffling from within the library.

'Hello?!' she called, feeling more hopeful. 'Can we come in to read some books please?'

'Sweet, sweet sorrow . . .'

whispered a sad, deep voice that Amelia didn't recognise.

'What the bats?' squeaked Grimaldi.

Amelia raised an eyebrow. 'Um, hello?' she said to the closed doors again, knocking one last time.

'Wait!' came another voice from behind her.

Everyone swung round to see a mummy maid with curly hair pushing a wheelbarrow full of books. Amelia remembered that she had met this particular mummy maid before, when she and Tangine had been on a mission to save the kingdom's lost memories.

'Hi Karl!' Amelia said with a wave. 'Can we please use the library? We heard voices inside, but no one's answering us.'

Karl looked scared. 'No go, no go! Not allowed in!' he said.

Florence frowned. 'WHY NOT?'

'These books safe,' said Karl, pointing a bandaged finger at the full wheelbarrow. Then he pointed towards the library doors and added, 'Those books not safe. Bad things in there!'

'Bad things?' whispered Grimaldi, his

empty eye-sockets wide with fear. Squashy bounced out of Amelia's arms and sniffed at the bottom of the door before giving a high-pitched squeak and hiding behind Amelia's legs.

'Dangerous things!' Karl cried, flinging his arms out so dramatically one of them nearly fell off. '*B- b-book . . .*'

'The *books* are dangerous?' asked Amelia, puzzled.

'No, no . . .' Karl took a deep breath and said quite clearly: '*Bookworms!*'

CHAPTER 4

I BET THEY COULDN'T EAT ME!

Amelia, Florence, Grimaldi and – eventually – Tangine gathered in one of the palace living rooms.

'Loose Limbs Library has been infested with bookworms, so Dad had to close it,' huffed Tangine grumpily. He had been unceremoniously shuffled down to the West Wing to greet his friends by a plum-stained Mable.

'It's such a shame,' said King Vladimir, entering the living room with a dramatic swish of his cape. 'Did Tangine not mention the bookworm incident to you at school?'

Tangine rolled his eyes and tightened the

belt on his silky dressing gown. 'Dad, I have SO much to think about already, like remembering to get out of bed, or eat my breakfast or take care of my nails and my hair and MY COMPLEXION. I can't remember *everything*.'

'CAN'T YOU JUST TELL THESE BOOKWORMS TO SHOVE OFF?' asked Florence.

'It's not as simple as that.' King Vladimir sighed. 'When they infest, well . . . that's the END for a library.'

'But what exactly do bookworms *do*?' asked Amelia, still feeling very confused.

'THIS,' said Tangine, holding up a book of classic pixie tales with a HUGE bite mark taken out of it. 'This was one of Mum's favourites.

She found it half-eaten in the library last week. Since then more and more books have had chunks bitten out of them, so Dad evacuated the mummy maids' stray limbs that worked in there and we've not been in since.'

Amelia widened her eyes. She could hardly believe it!

'WAIT . . .' said Florence, taking the half-munched book. 'THE BOOKWORMS EAT BOOKS?'

'Indeed. And once they start, there's no stopping them!' said the king.

'Surely we can do *something*?' asked Grimaldi. 'It seems crazy to shut down a WHOLE library just because of a few *worms* . . .'

'Oh, they don't *just* eat books, Grimaldi. They eat ANYTHING that gets in their way!' said Tangine. He walked right up to Grimaldi so that they were almost nose to skull. 'They'd eat YOU if you got close enough!'

Grimaldi yelped.

'OH, COME ON,' said Florence, picking

Tangine up by the head and moving him to one side. 'I BET THEY COULDN'T EAT ME!' She marched out of the living room. 'LET'S SEE 'OW THESE WORMS FEEL ABOUT A RARE BREED OF YETI, EH?!'

'I really would advise you NOT to go into the library!' called King Vladimir.

But Florence was already gone.

Amelia ran out after Florence as she headed towards the library's closed doors. She was with Florence on this one. How could a few bookworms cause so much trouble? They were just WORMS, after all.

'TRAGEDY! CALAMITY! MISFORTUNE! DISAAAAASTEEEEEER!'

It was the sad, deep voice again. But this time, it was louder and much more melodramatic. Amelia skidded to a halt next to Florence.

Florence placed a wary paw on one of the door handles.

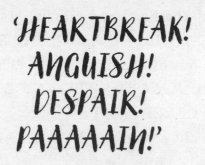

'HEARTBREAK! ANGUISH! DESPAIR! PAAAAAIN!'

'I DUNNO IF WE SHOULD GO IN THERE . . .' said Florence.

'Maybe the bookworm is in pain?' said Amelia. 'Maybe it needs our help?'

'HOPELESS!
HURT...'

'See?' said Amelia.

She reached past Florence for the door handle. But then, much MUCH louder than before, the deep voice yelled once again, making the library doors shudder.

'...TORMENT,
DEATH.'

Amelia let her raised hand drop to her side.

'Err, maybe you're right,' she said, backing away from the library and pulling Florence with her.

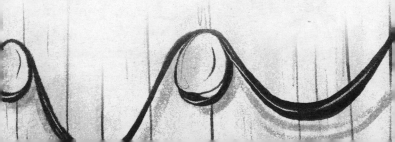

CHAPTER 5

MORE OF AN EGGSHELL

Amelia and her friends decided to sit together and do their story-writing homework in Tangine's bedroom. Amelia tucked herself in the corner so that nobody would notice that she *still* hadn't started her story. Most of the pages in her notebook were either scratched-out ideas, doodles of pumpkins, or splodges of brain-pie. Amelia had been counting on the library to give her inspiration. Now that it was out of bounds, she wasn't sure what to do!

Her mother's words rang through her head. *Don't be afraid to ask for a little help if you need it, my little fart-fest.*

NO! Amelia thought to herself. *Everyone's expecting me to come up with a good story. I shouldn't need help from anyone!* She shook her head and chewed at the end of her bat-wing pen anxiously.

'I'M ALREADY HALF-WAY FRU MY ADVENTURE STORY!' cheered Florence.

'That's great, Florence!' said Grimaldi, who was curled up on Tangine's bed with his notebook.

'I'm about to write the most TRAGIC moment in mine,' Tangine sang, then pretended to fall on the floor and die.

Amelia didn't say anything.

'AMELIA?' said Florence, edging up to her friend. 'YOU'RE VERY QUIET AND YOU LOOK A BIT PALE . . . AS IN, PALER THAN YOUR USUAL VAMPIRE PALENESS.'

'Yeah, you're a little grey around the edges,' Grimaldi added.

'I'd say she looks more *eggshell*,' said Tangine, taking hold of Amelia's chin and studying her face. 'In fact, your complexion is *quite* awful, but I can sort that RIGHT out for you. I have some of my EveryKing Sparkles cheek cream in my Drawer of Creams . . .'

'SHE DON'T WANT NONE OF YOUR CHEEKIN' CREAM,' said Florence, shoving Tangine out of the way. 'WHAT'S UP, AMELIA?'

Amelia closed her notebook. 'Nothing,' she said with a fake, fang-filled smile. 'Just thinking about my story.'

'WELL, I CAN'T WAIT TO 'EAR IT,' said Florence. She put a big hairy arm around Amelia's shoulders and hugged her tight. 'ALL THIS WRITIN' IS MAKIN' ME PRETTY 'UNGRY THOUGH!'

'Oooh! Shaun the mummy maid makes the BEST armpit sweatshakes,' said Tangine. 'I'll get him to make some for us and we can read our stories to each other! It'll be divine.

Oh, and TRAGIC of course.'

'It'll be tragic, all right,' Amelia muttered to herself quietly.

Whilst Shaun the mummy maid brewed the armpit sweatshakes, Amelia decided to take a little walk around the palace on her own. How could she share her story with her friends when she hadn't even started writing it?!

'I'm just going to the toilet,' she said, popping her notebook in her pocket.

Tangine waved a hand. 'Don't use the one on the fifth floor,' he said. 'One of the mummy maids' legs fell down it and now its blocked.'

Amelia trudged down the quiet and long shiny corridors of Nocturnia Palace. The Loose Limbs Library lay ahead of her, and Amelia became lost in a world of thoughts about all the wonderful stories that had been eaten by the Bookworms.

'THE FULL MOON ROSE!'

The words boomed loudly down the silent corridor, almost knocking Amelia off her feet in surprise. It was coming from inside the library.

Amelia crept closer to the library doors.

'AND THE BEAUTIFUL PUMPKIN QUEEN RETURNED!'

Amelia gasped. 'Wait a minute,' she said to herself. 'That's a line from my one of favourite Nocturnian tales . . .'

Amelia's curiosity got the better of her. She carefully pulled away the black ribbon, took a deep breath and, as quietly as she could, pushed the door open.

CREEEEEEEEEEEEEEEEEEEEAAAAAAK!

Amelia winced. She really wished every door in Nocturnia didn't creak so much. She held her breath for a second and listened for any movement.

Silence.

She slipped
through the
door and tiptoed
into the seemingly
empty library, making
her way over to a scattered
pile of books. She spotted a copy
of *The Pumpkin Whisperer* – her favourite
book – lying open on the floor and picked it
up. There was a huge bite-shaped hole right
through the middle of it.

Something wet and slimy suddenly dripped
on to Amelia's hand. A long dark shadow
stretched across the room.

Amelia looked up very slowly.

Two large, bright eyes shone out of the
darkness. A large drooling mouth opened
wide, displaying hundreds of sharp little
teeth with bits of pages stuck in
all the gaps.

It was a bookworm.

CHAPTER 6

MAGIC AND WONDER

'*AAAAAAAAAAAAAAAAAAAAAAAAA AAAARGH!*'

Amelia ran as fast as she could, weaving in and out of the bookshelves before throwing herself behind a huge stack of half-eaten books. She hugged her knees into her chest and sat as still as possible, which was hard to do when you were trembling with fear. What if Tangine was right? Maybe the bookworm *did* want to eat her!

She could hear something slithering along the carpet nearby. She peeked from behind the pile of books to see if there was any way out.

A bookworm with a frilly collar was sitting right in front of the library door, munching

34

contentedly on a very old and expensive-looking first edition of *The Tale of Two Turnips*.

How the bats was she going to escape without getting eaten? Amelia nervously flicked the tattered pages of *The Pumpkin Whisperer* back and forth as she tried to think of an idea.

That was it!

Taking one last, sad look at the half-eaten book, Amelia raised her arm and threw it as far as she could, AWAY from the door. She watched as the bookworm wiggled off at full speed towards the book, leaving a clear path to the door.

It was now or never. Amelia clambered to her feet and ran.

'WAIT!' someone called from behind her.

Amelia swung round and bumped into something with a great big BOMP!

'Ouch!' She fell back on her bottom, rubbing her head.

'*Golly gumdrops!*' said a strange voice.

Amelia looked up to see the bookworm

gazing at her. She opened her mouth to let out a loud scream, when something very unexpected happened.

The bookworm smiled.

'Little Vampire, you forgot to take your book with you,' said the bookworm, picking up the copy of *The Pumpkin Whisperer* with her tail and placing it gently into Amelia's lap. She straightened up so that the moonlight shone upon her pointy glasses and posh pointy collar.

'I see you like the stories of *The Pumpkin Whisperer* too?' the bookworm said, nodding at the half-eaten book. 'Isn't it just *perfection*?! It tastes like MAGIC and WONDER, with extra magic in chapter three and non-stop wonder in chapter ten. Those kinds of stories taste the BEST!'

Amelia was a little lost for words. 'I . . . er, yes,' she said, clutching the book nervously. 'This is my one of *my* favourites too! Although, I'm not entirely sure what it *tastes* like.'

The bookworm wriggled with excitement. 'Oh, it's GLORIOUS! And the *pictures* . . . there's nothing like them! They add so much depth to the flavour. My favourite is the one of the Pumpkin Queen dancing around the glowing pumpkin patch!'

Suddenly, another large bookworm emerged from between the bookshelves and slithered over. This one had a curly moustache, thick round glasses and a bow tie.

'Finally! Another creature we can talk to about BOOKS!' said the worm. 'I'm Percival,' he told Amelia with a bow of his head. 'I see you've met my wife, Penelope. Oh, and these are our children . . . Kids!' he called out.

Three little bookworms wiggled into the moonlight next to their parents. It was a whole bookworm family!

The biggest of the three, wearing a leather jacket and a spiky collar, grinned cheekily at Amelia. 'Prue's the name!'

Her little sister bobbed up and down excitedly next to her. 'Hi, I'm Poppy!' she said, as her unicorn headband slipped over one eye.

The youngest bookworm slid behind his mother and peeked out at Amelia.

'This is Pod,' Penelope said, affectionately. 'He's a little bit shy.'

'Hello,' said Amelia with a small wave. 'I'm Amelia Fang.'

'Oh, what's this?' asked Penelope, using her tail to pick up a small book splayed out on the floor next to Amelia. 'It looks VERY tasty indeed.'

It was Amelia's notebook.

CHAPTER 7

A DASH OF DEATH

Percival sniffed the edge of Amelia's notebook. 'Hmmm, it smells like a story just waiting to happen!' he said. 'How exciting! I wonder what it TASTES like . . .'

Percival opened his mouth, ready to take a BIG bite out of the notebook.

'Wait!' Amelia said quickly, making the worms jump. 'Um . . .

that's actually
my book.'

'Oooh, how
wonderful!'
Penelope beamed.
Amelia sighed.
'It's not, really.'

'Mummy,' said
Pod quietly, tugging
at Penelope's tail.
'Why does the vampire look sad?'

Penelope leaned in closer to the tiny
bookworm and smiled. 'Why don't you ask
her yourself?'

Pod blushed. Slinking slowly up to Amelia,
he asked shyly, 'Why do you look sad,
Amelia Fang?'

Amelia decided to tell the truth. 'Well, I'm
meant to be writing a story . . .' she began.

'IS IT TRAGIC?!' asked Prue with
excitement.

'Let her finish, dear!' said Penelope sternly.

Amelia took a deep breath. 'Well, it's a
little tragic because I can't think of what to

write. I'm usually great at thinking of ideas, and my friends *and* my teacher are expecting an amazing story from me. But I'm just going to end up looking really silly in front of my class because I can't think of *anything*.'

'That *is* a bit tragic,' said Prue. Then she grinned. 'But it doesn't have to END that way, does it?'

Now she'd spoken her fears out loud, Amelia felt as if a heavy weight had been lifted from her shoulders. 'What do you mean?' she asked.

'Maybe talking through your ideas with us would help,' Penelope suggested.

Amelia wasn't so sure. 'But surely I shouldn't *need* to ask for help?'

'PISH POSH!' Percival blustered. 'Everyone needs help sometimes! And it's not like we're writing it FOR you.' He lowered his glasses with his tail and raised an eyebrow. 'We can't write anyway.'

'We can't even *read*,' Poppy added.

'*You're not meant to tell anyone that!*' snapped Prue.

'Okay girls, calm down,' urged their mother.

'You can't read?' Amelia asked curiously.

Percival smiled. 'It's not so bad,' he said. 'That's why we *eat* the books; to get a *taste* for the story instead!'

'I see,' Amelia said as it all began to make sense. 'You know, other creatures wouldn't be so scared of you if they knew that's why you ate the books.'

Pod looked at Amelia with big sad eyes. 'We're too em-babba-rassed . . .'

Penelope gave Pod a hug with her tail. 'Pod's right. We're too *embarrassed* to tell anyone that we can't read. Like you and your story, we're worried about what others might think of us. But it turns out they're too scared to talk to us anyway! So, we're in a bit of a pickle.'

A brilliant idea suddenly came to Amelia. 'Well, how would you like to *learn* to read?' she asked. 'I could help you. Then you wouldn't need to eat the books any more!'

The bookworms looked at each other with

shocked expressions. Amelia really hoped she hadn't offended them.

'Why, that's . . .' Percival began.

'A WONDROUS IDEA!' finished Penelope.

Amelia laughed as Poppy spun on the spot with excitement and Pod did a roly-poly straight into a bookshelf. 'And I'll tell EVERYONE how lovely you really are!' she added.

Penelope's eyes welled up. 'You'd do that for us?'

'Of course!' Amelia exclaimed. 'The kingdom needs to know that you're as friendly and welcoming as any other vampire, yeti or unicorn!'

'I love unicorns!' sang Poppy. 'And I REALLY like comics about unicorns! And toads!' She waggled her unicorn-horn headband happily and used it to point at one of the comic books on the floor. The corners of the comic had been munched. 'The tastiest ones are the action-packed adventures. But I can't WAIT to be able to read them instead.'

'I think you'd get on very well with my

friend Florence,' said Amelia with a giggle. 'She loves reading adventure comics too!'

Prue picked up a small black book with her tail. She took a long sniff along the length of the book's spine. 'ROMANCE *and* TRAGEDY,' she said dramatically, in a deep, sad voice. 'That's what makes a book taste good. Add some *disaster* and a dash of *death*, and you're in for the most DELICIOUS story ever.'

Amelia threw her arms up in the air. 'It's YOUR voice we could hear shouting about disaster and death in the library yesternight!' she said. 'My friend Tangine loves those kinds of books too.'

Amelia really loved talking to the bookworms. But then all the chatting stopped as a loud scream echoed through Loose Limbs Library.

CHAPTER 8
LLAMA QUEEN

'THEY'VE EATEN AMELIA!!!'

The sound of Tangine's shrieking caused all the bookworms to slither away and hide in the depths of the bookshelves. Tangine burst into the library, waving his arms around and running straight past Amelia.

'Wait! Tangine! Stop!' Amelia shouted. 'I'm very much alive! LOOK! I'm HERE. I've *not* been eaten!'

'That's what they WANT US TO THINK!' Tangine shrieked hysterically.

A flustered Grimaldi came floating into the library next, followed by a bounding Florence, with Squashy and Pumpy pa-doinging and pa-doofing behind her.

'FANK THE SERPENTS YOU'RE ALL RIGHT, AMELIA,' Florence puffed. 'WHEN YOU NEVVA CAME BACK FROM THE TOILET, WE GOT SO WORRIED. NOBODY TAKES THAT LONG EVEN WHEN THEY'RE DOING A BIG P—'

'OOOOOOKAY!' Amelia interrupted, holding both hands up in the air. 'Enough everyone! There's been a BIG misunderstanding. Guys . . . I've met the bookworms!'

Tangine gasped, looking like he might faint at any moment. Florence and Grimaldi looked at her in horror.

'It's okay!' Amelia said cheerfully as Squashy leapt into her arms and began to lick her cheeks. 'The bookworms mean us no harm. All they're interested in eating is *books*. Nothing else.'

'But how do you know that's true?' squeaked Grimaldi, who was hiding behind Florence.

'See for yourself,' said Amelia.

She beckoned to the bookworms to come back out into the moonlight. Florence, Grimaldi and Tangine stepped backwards warily, almost falling over a cowering Pumpy. Safe in the arms of Amelia, Squashy waggled his little pumpkin stalk from side to side.

Penelope gasped in delight. 'Oh! I've never been this close to a REAL-LIFE pumpkin before!' She slithered a little closer to Squashy and Amelia. 'I've only tasted books about them.'

'SO, YOU DON'T WANNA EAT US?' asked Florence gingerly.

'No, Large Rare Breed of Yeti, we do not!' proclaimed Percival. 'We only eat books. Plus, you wouldn't taste good anyway.'

'I'M NOT SURE IF I'M RELIEVED OR OFFENDED BY THAT,' said Florence.

'The bookworms eat books because . . .' Amelia began, before turning to the bookworms. 'Is it okay for me to say?'

Prue slithered forward and announced bravely, 'We eat the books because we can't read.'

'You can't READ?' said Tangine, looking baffled. 'But how does EATING books help you?'

Prue leaned across to a half-eaten pile of books and picked up a copy of *The Love and Loss of a Llama Queen* in her mouth. She dropped it at Tangine's feet. 'Because it *tastes* like LOVE, PASSION and TRAGEDY,' she said seriously.

Tangine squeaked in delight. 'LLAMA QUEEN! I LOVE this book!'

'But *reading* these books would be much better!' said Penelope. 'Especially as that means that everyone can still enjoy the books.' She bowed her head. 'We never meant to ruin your library. It's just packed FULL of delicious stories and we couldn't resist!'

'I was thinking that we could help the bookworms to learn to read?' Amelia suggested to her friends.

'Ooo! Well, we're writing our own stories for our homework,' said Grimaldi. He'd finally floated out from behind Florence, putting his scythe discreetly back in the folds of his black cloak. 'Maybe we could all read our stories out loud with the bookworms? That might be a good start.'

Amelia twisted her hands together anxiously. In all the excitement of discovering how wonderful the bookworms really were, she had forgotten that she hadn't yet written her own story.

'And WE can help you with *your* story, Little Vampire,' said Penelope kindly, noticing the change in her new friend.

'HUH?' Florence piped up. 'AMELIA, I FORT YOU HAD ALREADY WRITTEN YOUR STORY?'

Amelia looked at the floor. 'Nope,' she whispered. 'I couldn't think of anything, and the more I tried, the more frustrated I became and the emptier my brain got.'

'OH, AMELIA,' said Florence. 'YOU

SHOULD'VE SAID SUMFIN' SOONER. WE
COULD 'AVE 'ELPED YOU.'

'Exactly,' Grimaldi added. 'You *always*
help us out. Friends are there to help
each other!'

Amelia sighed. 'I was worried that you
might be disappointed in me and think I
sounded silly,' she said.

'NEVER!' said Tangine theatrically. 'We don't think that. THINKING you sound silly *is silly*!' He winked and gave his friend a big glittery hug.

'Really?' said Amelia, feeling relieved.

'I'm always asking for your help with stuff,' said Grimaldi. 'Do you think *I'm* silly?'

'Absolutely not!' protested Amelia.

'Well there you go!' said Grimaldi. Then he frowned and stroked his chin. 'I think I just gave wise advice . . . *Did I just give wise advice*?' he said, looking half-shocked and half-pleased with himself.

Percival nodded solemnly. 'You are wise, indeed, Little Grim Reaper.'

Amelia felt something wrap around her shoulders and saw Penelope's big friendly face.

'We are all so much happier now, thanks to you. You have shown us bookworms not to be ashamed to ask for help. And you shouldn't be either,' Penelope said.

'EMBRACE THE FEAR,' said Prue.

'EMBRACE THE DEATH!' Tangine cried.

Everyone looked at him.

'Actually,' Tangine quickly added, 'don't do that.'

Amelia giggled. If the bookworms could be brave enough to ask for help, then so could she!

CHAPTER 9

THE WHOLE (NOT VERY) TRAGIC TALE

For the rest of the night, everyone worked together to tidy the library and gather up as many non-munched books as possible to read with the bookworms.

Amelia read out book after book about pumpkins and magic to a spellbound Penelope, whilst Florence and Poppy whizzed through pages of action-packed comics. Grimaldi read nice, calming poems to Pod who had taken a big shine to the little grim reaper and was snuggled up close to him.

'I'm so happy to have found someone who loves pumpkins as much as I do!' said Penelope. 'I bet you could write a wonderful pumpkin-themed story.'

'I'd love to write a story about pumpkins,' said Amelia. 'I just don't know what would happen in the story.'

'Why don't you use what's right in front of you for inspiration?' Penelope suggested, nodding towards Amelia's friends. 'Your own pumpkin, your friends, the flamboyant fairy prince!'

Tangine was swooning and beating his brow to accompany the passionate and tragic stories he was sharing with Prue.

'I think you might be right,' Amelia said. 'We've been on so many adventures together, I could write about those . . . and any bits I get stuck on, I could ask the others to help because they were there, too!'

'Sounds delicious!' said Penelope with a wink.

'Thank you,' said Amelia. 'For helping me to find my writing spark again.'

Penelope leaned over Amelia's shoulder with a big smile. 'And thank you for making my family so happy, Amelia. You encouraged us to talk about our worries, and I would love to hear the story YOU have written once it is finished.'

'Would you like to come to my school on Monday night and listen to me read it to the rest of the class?' Amelia asked bravely.

'Oh, *can we, can we*?!' asked Pod, tugging at his mother's tail.

'We would LOVE that! But are you sure your school friends won't be scared of us?' asked Penelope.

'WE'RE GONNA TELL THEM ALL THE TRUTH ABOUT 'OW LOVELY YOU ARE!' declared Florence.

'Yes,' agreed Tangine. 'The whole (*not very*) TRAGIC tale!'

Amelia grinned. 'We definitely have some stories that we need to tell . . . to the whole of Nocturnia!'

At Catacomb Academy's Abominable Assembly on Monday night, Amelia's class stood at the back of the hall as they waited to read out their stories to each other. Amelia felt a little nervous.

'YOU OKAY, AMELIA?' Florence whispered to her friend. 'YOU GOT THIS!'

'Yeah, just pretend we're a library full of bookworms,' said Grimaldi.

'Or a room full of *Tangines*,' suggested Tangine.

Amelia giggled despite the flutter bats in her tummy.

'*Amelia Fang!*' rang out the voice of the head teacher, Miss Inspine.

Amelia took a deep breath and walked bravely to the front of the hall. Her hands were a bit shaky as she opened her notebook, but her heart swelled when she

saw all her best friends sitting there, including the very excited bookworm family. Amelia cleared her throat and began to read.

'*It was a dark and gloomy Wednesday night in Nocturnia . . .*'

The class was spellbound as Amelia told her story about pumpkins dressed as daisies, pompous wishing-wells, jolly mermaid-leprechauns, magical sugarplums and naughty caticorns. It felt like hardly any time had passed before Amelia spoke the very last words of her story:

'*The End!*'

Amelia beamed as the hall burst into applause.

'Now I bet that story would taste *extraordinary*!' Penelope called out happily.

The pupils of Catacomb Academy fell silent, and all eyes turned to the friendly-

looking bookworm. Penelope lowered her pointy glasses and winked at the puzzled-looking students.

'But I would much rather READ it!' she said.

AMELIA FANG

Join the little
vampire with a big heart
for some howlingly hilarious adventures!

Sam Wu is not afraid of ANYTHING. Well,
apart from ghosts, sharks, the dark, spiders . . .
but definitely not ZOMBIES!

Read on for a taste of this brilliantly
funny book, out now!

CONFESSIONS IN THE CRAFT CORNER

It all started when I noticed that Ralph and Regina kept falling asleep in class.

Ralph might be my nemesis, but I didn't want Regina to get in trouble, so I threw a balled up piece of paper at her head to wake her up. It just bounced off her, and she kept sleeping.

"Regina!" I whispered as loud as I dared. Nothing. Ralph drooled a little bit next to her.

"Regina!" I tried again. No response.

When our teacher Ms Winkleworth turned back to the board, I threw an eraser at Regina.

Unfortunately, I don't have great aim. The eraser hit Ralph instead.

"Ow!" he said, jolting awake and rubbing the

back of his head. Regina must have heard him, because she woke up too, blinking sleepily. Ralph looked around and saw me staring straight at him. Then he threw the eraser back, *way* harder than I had.

"Ow!" I said, as the eraser hit me in the nose.

"What is going on?" said Ms Winkleworth, who had turned around just in time to see the eraser bounce off my nose. "Ralph, are you throwing things?"

"Sam Wu threw his eraser at me first!" said Ralph.

Sam, is that true?" said Ms Winkleworth, staring me down.

I wanted to explain that it was because Ralph and Regina had been sleeping and I was trying to help, but I didn't want to be a tattler (even though Ralph had just told on me). So I tried to be the bigger person and just shrugged. "It was an accident," I said. "It just . . . flew out of my hands. Like magic."

"Maybe it was a ghost!" said Bernard, who always has my back. He is one of my best friends and is the smartest person I know. He's basically a walking dictionary.

"*Exactly*," I said, giving Ms Winkleworth my most serious face.

Ms Winkleworth sighed. "Sam, erasers don't just fly out of people's hands," she said. Then she went and wrote both of our names on the board and circled them. "You two will both have to stay inside today at break and help tidy the craft corner."

"That's not fair," Ralph whined. "Sam Wu started it."

"Well, next time you should both think twice about throwing erasers in class," said Ms Winkleworth.

❧

And that was how I found myself in the craft corner with my nemesis, Ralph Zinkerman the Third.

"You should do the tidying," he said when Ms Winkleworth was at her desk going through some papers. "This is your fault!"

"I was trying to help you!" I spluttered.

"Well, I was trying to help Regina, but you were asleep too! I could have told on you, you know.

But I didn't." I held my head a little higher
when I said this.

I was not asleep!

Ralph said.

**You were!
And you drooled.**

"I do **NOT** drool," Ralph said with a snort.
He is the master of snorts.

"You did," I said. Then I frowned. "Why are
you both so tired recently?"

Ralph sighed and sat down. "None of your
business," he said as he held back a yawn. "And
I'm not tired."

"I'm just trying to help," I said.

"Why?" said Ralph suspiciously.

I had to think about that one. It was true, Ralph was my nemesis. He *always* made fun of me in front of everyone and he called me names like Scaredy Cat Sam and Sam Wu-ser (which he thinks is funny because he makes my last name sound like loser).

But even if Ralph wasn't always my friend, Regina was. And I had a feeling that whatever was bothering Ralph would be bothering her too. Plus, I'd learned from SPACE BLASTERS that sometimes being a good Captain is checking in on all of your crew, even the ones you don't like as much.

"Because we're in the same crew," I said.

Ralph snorted (like I said, he is the master

of snorts) and rolled his eyes. "That was one camping trip in the woods," he said. "And don't think it means we're best friends or anything now. Because we're not."

"Suit yourself," I said, and turned to organize some paint brushes. I tried to whistle too, to show how much I wasn't bothered, but I don't know how to whistle, so instead I kind of just blew air out of my mouth and hooted a bit.

"Why are you making train noises?" Ralph said. "You are so weird."

"I'm just whistling," I said. "Minding my own business."

Ralph scowled. "Fine! I'll tell you. Regina will probably tell you anyway. She's convinced that you and your friends are the only ones who can help us. I don't know why."

"Really?" I said, standing up a little straighter. It was nice to feel appreciated.

Ralph paused and then looked around to make sure nobody could hear him.

"Do you remember what Regina said is trapped in our basement?"

I gulped. Ralph couldn't be talking about what I thought he was talking about . . . could he?

"You don't mean . . . " I couldn't even say it.

Ralph nodded solemnly.

"It's louder than ever. We can't sleep at night because we're worried it's going to get out."

I gulped again.

"And eat us," he added, in case it wasn't clear. "We don't know what to do."

"Well," I said, trying to show how brave I was even though I was starting to sweat, "the first thing we need to do is to get everyone in our crew back together if we're going to face ... **THE ZOMBIE WEREWOLF**."

Well **hello** there! We are

Overjoyed that you have **joined our celebration** of

Reading books and **sharing stories**, because we

Love bringing **books** to you.

Did you know, we are a **charity** dedicated to celebrating the

Brilliance of **reading for pleasure** for everyone, everywhere?

Our mission is to help you discover **brand new stories** and

Open your mind to exciting **new worlds** and characters, from

Kings and **queens** to **wizards** and **pirates** to **animals** and **adventurers** and so many more. We couldn't

Do it without all the amazing **authors** and **illustrators**, **booksellers** and **bookshops**, publishers, schools and **libraries** out there –

And most importantly, we couldn't do it all without . . .

YOU!

On your bookmarks, get set, READ! Happy Reading. Happy World Book Day.

Rob Biddulph

SHARE A STORY

From breakfast to bedtime, there's always time to discover and share stories together. You can...

1 TAKE A TRIP to your LOCAL BOOKSHOP

Brimming with brilliant books and helpful booksellers to share awesome reading recommendations, you can also enjoy booky events with your favourite authors and illustrators.

FIND YOUR LOCAL BOOKSHOP: booksellers.org.uk/ bookshopsearch

2 JOIN your LOCAL LIBRARY

That wonderful place where the hugest selection of books you could ever want to read awaits – and you can borrow them for FREE! Plus expert advice and fantastic free family reading events.

FIND YOUR LOCAL LIBRARY: gov.uk/local-library-services/

3 CHECK OUT the WORLD BOOK DAY WEBSITE

Looking for reading tips, advice and inspiration? There is so much for you to discover at **worldbookday.com**, packed with fun activities, games, downloads, podcasts, videos, competitions and all the latest new books galore.

SPONSORED BY

NATIONAL BOOK tokens

Rob Biddulph

Celebrate stories. Love reading.

World Book Day is a registered charity funded by publishers and booksellers in the UK & Ireland.